Herja, Devastation

Frank Prem
&
Cage Dunn

Herja, Devastation is a tale of

myth and mortality,

wielder and implement,

love and destiny.

Free-verse poetry combines with short prose in the style of
an Eddic tale modernised.

* * *

The legend of Valkyrie breathes,
as Herja, Devastation, once wronged,
aims her mortal agent at her enemies.

Her man bears this tale of vengeance in service
to a higher, eminently more noble being.
He is her assassin and tool, and she is
his destiny and dignity.

In the dirty business of death on demand,
a purity of purpose lights the path
as he seeks questions, provides answers
and justice on her word.

This blending of literary forms creates a unique nouveau
noir style for the 21st Century.

Do you dare to tread the dark side?

service

I was a man
once

never forget it

what sort of man?
.
.
.

not much
I don't suppose
but still ...

I stood
and I stood
alone
needed no one

wanted nothing
at all
except
my wits

I always had
my wits
about me

it was my wits
that kept me sharp
it was
my wits
that kept me
ahead
of others

even when I knew
it was
all up
for me

with nowhere to go
and no way of escaping
even then
I knew that I had done
everything
one man could do
with wit

I didn't ask for her
to save me

I did not
once
raise my eyes
in a plea

but
she came
like a fire from the gods

she came
like nemesis
singing

and wit?

I'd no wit
at all
no mind no brain
only addle

she took me

she claimed me

and my wit
is nothing
now
but another word
for service

*A man who walks in the shade has
a darker shadow for company.*

CONTENTS

1.

POW! for the job

you have to
know
your guy

when he wakes
what he does

when he leaves home
in the morning

when he's going
to get back

even
when he uses the crapper

you have to know
the guy

who
is his wife
or his girl

or his guy

who does he go
to the football game
with

when does the light
get turned off
at night

it's like
you almost have to be
him

I know I know
it sounds all
pseudo-freud

pop-gun psychology

I know
but
I ask you

how can you bump him
if you don't
know him

POW!

you have to
know him

that's the job

The call comes in, a simple message. Doesn't mean much. Meet me, the text says. And I go, but not to her, not yet. The package arrives, the work begins.

Assess the situation, the environment, and calculate.

First, always first, comes the basic stuff. The plan, the preparation, the first watch. Assess the situation, calculate the trajectories and options from the paths people take, the maps they make. I prepare.

I'll know when it comes, the need to dig deep, to find the place and time to act.

It's the next stage of the yarn. The visage. Shape the outer to meet the need of the inner. See with more than eyes, feel with more than touch, taste it all, absorb every nuance. Extrapolate from the surroundings. Become. I bury the person some may think they know. I become.
And then I move in. As visible as the shadow of a single eucalyptus leaf. I become.

For someone the final moment awaits.

Who is this person? That's what I needs to know.

The things he leaves out is what I use; cans down the side of the house, bins with secrets hid, cars and sheds and boxes what's got their lives all tucked inside. I reads 'em, finds out what they does, who they does it with, where they go, and I wait, like a desert scorpion, under the sand, set the ambush, mark time for the moment of intense shadows, when opportunity slides up close, and I gotta go do the job fast and neat.

To find out who he is, my task, this man, he got a wife? Or a girl? Or a boy? Or all three? Gotta know all these bits, gotta know where they hide, what they hide, how they hide. All while behind the mask, nothin' but sounds and shapes and colours that ain't the real me.

No two-ups, no second chance. The job goes one way or t'other, and all up to me which way for each.

How I gets here, where I sits, how I hold my breath when I steals the clothes from the charities, from the collection bins, slips into 'em, take on the fake mask, an' slides aroun' the cars in the street, become one with the invisible things. One bottle I holds, empty, of course, but I swings it when someone comes in too near, and they go, sometimes a'mutterin', sometimes a'swearin', but they never come back, they never look twice.

Skin is dirty, hair lank, the stinky shirt, and dogs be thanked with a packet of 'roo bits, a kind hand, and I's in there with the street dogs, the mongrels, invisible to all but the noses.

I sits with me tongue restin' on the floor of me mouth, and I breathes slow and calm while the body leans in such-like, and no one ever sees the drunks on the road, or tucked in the alleys, or scroungin' in the filth, do they?

And I wait to see 'im. The one what's got 'is name on the paper. What if they's real dumb and don't hide? All the easier, it seems. But these ones she sends me to, they all be hiders, they all look over the shoulder, see if they can see what ain't there.

That be me. I don't got no baggage, nothing to hold me to a place or time. And the face they see? Invisible, one of the lost ghouls, on the skids. Better not to see those, or's else they catch it, become it. Do they get a creepy tingle down the back? When their name is on my list, and I comes for 'em, do they sense it? Do they know? Does the tickin' in me head warn them?

Nah. They never see me. Not then.

when it's done

me?

I like
a little distance

a rifle
a suppressor
a good scope

sometimes though
mostly
it's up close

a snub nose
at the back of the head

in and out
with a blade

once
it was the wire
but
it's not possible
to keep your stress levels
down
with the wire

it's too physical

I get
a little blood pressure

no need
to tell the boss
but
I don't like it
when I can feel my heart
banging
inside me

an accident
is the absolute best
I suppose
but that's not always possible
to arrange

I just do
what I have to do

when a job's done
it's done

It's only at the right time, when they gotta know what's a'comin' to 'em, that's when they knows. I don't like up close, but she says what's gotta be, how it goes, if its gotta be that way. If they gotta know why, that's how it goes.

I gets told how. She's the boss. She says who, she says how.

Not when, 'cos only my part will do for that, but iffen she wants it distant, out comes the .308, kept safe and ready, with the two messages.

Nah, I don't miss, but we gotta be sure, ya know. Gotta be sure.

Proper prep is professional, so I has two messages, two soft and shiny slugs, ready to sign on the line.

An' I gotta show proof for some, get a final shot, a last dot of the 'i' or cross of the 't'. Can I ask, I says, if you don't trust me to get the right one? But it's not that, just being professional, she says. Makes sure.

The up-close and personal stuff, the small things, easy to hide, easy to get to me, sometimes she leaves 'em, and I knows what she wants. I always knows what she wants from the gifts she leaves.

Piano-wire, and she wants him to sing into the recorder. Leaves a bloody mess, though, so I gotta make sure my good clothes is hid somewhere close and dry, and get a hose or a tub or a pool to clean it all up.

Mess is bad. No mess is good. Long shot better than hands-on. But a rifle means she's sent him a message already, he's been told. Not a warning, and he's waiting for me, for his end.

A bit of a problem sometimes, when they's so careful, but no one gets off, no one gets by.

Not if they're on her list.

Do I ever ask 'who was this person?' No. Once they're written in with ink, they's gonna be crossed off the list, I don't ask.

Don't get on that list, is what I says.

carry all

one suitcase

well
it's actually
a hand luggage
zip bag
with a shoulder sling

twenty inches long
and ten inches
deep
as specified by the airlines

that way
I can stow it
in the overhead locker

usually
I'm just in
and out
so traveling light
makes sense

sometimes I'm out
in a hurry
if you know
what I mean

no time wasted
packing

see
generally
someone meets me
drives me around
points out
all the significant sights

who
is who

and provides me
with any
what
is what

do the job

dispose of the
to be disposed of

grab my bag
get out
of town

that's all

A few days here, a few days only, and it's all over and now's the time to get out. The mask comes off, the shadow becomes light. The voice comes clear, the tone changes, the face is clean, shaven and washed, a face jagged with laughter lines. I stand taller in good shoes. I am me again. The poet, the man of words, the visitor.

It's time to leave. The last part of the plan.

The bob-a-job who showed me around town when I got in takes me back to the airport. The show is over, and the people go home, back to where they came from.

A plane, the Bob thinks, will take me away. And I have the small pack, the luggage of the exact size for the overhead lockers. And I get out, smile at him, nod. But I stand there 'til he's gone. Not just a bit down the off-ramp. I watch the car all the way to the lights at the highway. The Bob knows nothing, it's just a bit of business to him. Paid to show me places and give me the key to the lock-box of goodies.

Look after the bushie, she tells 'em, he's a poet.

Nothing else.

The game is played, the price is paid, and the look on the face of the Bob is wary, alert. So it should be. But he knows nothing, not then, not now. Not from her, nor from me. The Bob might sense a job is done, but what he knows isn't me. He sees me run and fly away, and any Bob who blows the whistle ... I smile at the memory of a few wordy Bobs, now erased.

The lady trusts few, and none so much as she trusts me. No few Bobs can cut our bond.

2.

sex appeal

there's something prett . . .

sexy
about a trigger

the smoothness
and
the curve

that slow tension
that you feel
through your finger
as you start
to
squeeze

you can really
feel
it

I don't care
for recoil
much
but
that whole piece of equipment
with the blue-metal
barrel

have you ever looked
through one of those things

the rifling!

man

the brown-orange kind of
colour
in the glass
of the scope

it feels warm
and when I sight
with the instrumentation
built inside the thing
well

see . . .

squeeze . . .

drop

a whiff of cordite

brimstone
in the air

not really
but . . .

you know . . .

I've got
a bit of
an imagination

The smooth as silk texture, the smell of gun oil, the anticipation ... it's home, where I belong until she needs me. I can be the real me, as much as possible, that is, without her.

One woman, and one love, and they're not the same. The woman, well, she's the devil to some, vengeance incarnate, the one who uses scars on the soul to hold you still while your heart comes out for examination. Don't have a black heart, and she won't see you. Don't lurk in the shadows, and you won't feel her touch.

They don't know her like I do. Not the devil, more the hand of divine retribution. She'll pick up those injured in battle, and give them purpose. Holds them to the line, offers a path. My love has no fear of death or injury, she has no fear of the fields of battle, and swings through those places like she was in a bar.

What she offers the downtrodden, the broken, the lost – not an easy path, but direction and purpose – what more can we ask for?

That wasn't how she found me. I'm the one percenter. Different. I showed her the light the first time, but she took the purpose under her wing. Me.

And her name. I gave her the name. She wears her name with pride and flaunts it when required.

She's got style, she's got class, she's got me. I pay attention, I do what she wants, and what she wants from me is a job well done.

That's the other love.

A job well-done needs a structured mind, a plan, a laid out process. And a tool. Not just any tool, the right tool.

This job needs a tool that's as exciting as first-time sexual conquest. The courting, the shaping, the gentle touches. The smile.

I see the message, and if it includes two of these – see how smooth they are, how representative? Run a finger down the length of it, caress the chill of intent, the smell of purpose.

The gun and bullets are part of the message. Distance is what she wants, they already know to be wary, she's spoken to them, given them the word. The warning went out. What I hold in my hand is the promise.

My body shudders with pleasure as I pack the tools, as I review the mark, as I plan my seduction.

The excitement is just like a new love, a prospect. I've got the go-ahead, and I don't ask why. I can imagine well enough, and I have a heart, so when she says, 'this is why' I believe, always, that it will be better with them gone.

And it always is.

The sky is clear, like a storm has passed. The body is replete, post-orgasmic, satiated.

And I have the perfume, like a lover's smell on my hand, to be remembered long after the act.

I almost forgot ...

the way
they make those bullets

if I see pictures
of a missile
getting launched
by us
or the chinese

the koreans

my mind
goes straight
to an image
of loose bullets

if I get a chance
I want to hold one
feel it
right there

right then

yeh

The feel of it, sensual, smooth, tough – like her, like life, like what it takes to pay the ferryman. The flames have died down, become embers. The memory of it becomes better than sex, better than life. The act undertaken has freed a prisoner, shown proof of the end. It is over. Each breath becomes normal, the façade is replaced by life, by living in among others.

That's why I write it out, to remember – no, not them, it's the feel of it – each one. A line in a poem, or a drawing in the gutter, or a slash of charcoal across the white surface. Words, I use words. No names, no evidence, no setting.

Poetry is what I use. Words with the height and clang of a bell tower, with the force of a suppressed cannon. Feel it? The explosive relief, the clean-up, the 'de-capo' – a few words to express ... how it feels to fly with the wild-eyed mob, to circle the enemy, to come out victorious. Words, that's all. Ever wondered if a word can kill?

Just a word. Just words. Not about the job, as such, but the tools – I can write about the tools, how it feels. I can say it's a story, that I write from imagination, from other stories written by other people. But that Raven story ain't got nothing on these. No airy-fairy fears in these words. No Poe in my poetry.

These words are real.

I speak them, too, but not the reality of them. I speak them as fiction, to the brawlers at the pub, the ones who don't know the true me. Nothing they say or think touches the sides of who I am, nothing touches my heart like the needs of her purpose.

What they see is who they think I am. An old reprobate, I've been called. A fox, a dirty dog, a liar and cheat.

Okay, I may have used all of those faces, but that's not who I am.

One person knows who I am, but she's the one thing I don't write about.

Not her, never about her. That's not said, but it's the rules.

Herja, my other love, and the crescendo of her devastation to those who need reminding.

something to discuss

I've heard
some bad things
said

about guys . . .
well
about some guys
who sound as though
they might be a little bit
like me

doctors
psychologists

talk
as if their ideas
are facts
you know

sociopath and psychopath
don't come near me
though

I'm a model citizen

something a bit like
a janitor

a sanitary worker
taking refuse off
the streets

I wouldn't mind
having a little
conversation
with a psychologist
about that

The mark is done, the world returns to the usual slow pace for all. I go places, you know, to interact, to learn how people think, why they think like that, what they do, how they lie or cheat or steal. In my trade, you gotta know the face behind the mask, so I go to the drub, listen to the chit-chat.

They think they know all, think it takes a bad guy, that what they know is all there is to know.

The worst of them all is the doctor-types. Not real doctors, but chit-chatters, the ones who think 'talking about it' will rid the world of the trauma in the face they talk at, bore into like an excavator.

Psychs, is what I call them. Sykes, but I can't call them what I want to.

Scythes, is what they are. Fools with fake tools. They bend the main sheaf of wheat, weight it down so the field can't be seen easily. They don't know what's coming up from below, or the diseases let in by failing to remove the rotten spore. Their words cut the wrong stalk.

They don't see what lies beneath, what's buried, hidden from sight.

I do. She does. We fix it. One effort expended is all.

If one day she sends me to one of them specialist types, I wonder if he'd like a little enlightenment on the way out?

Am I the demon of which he dreams?

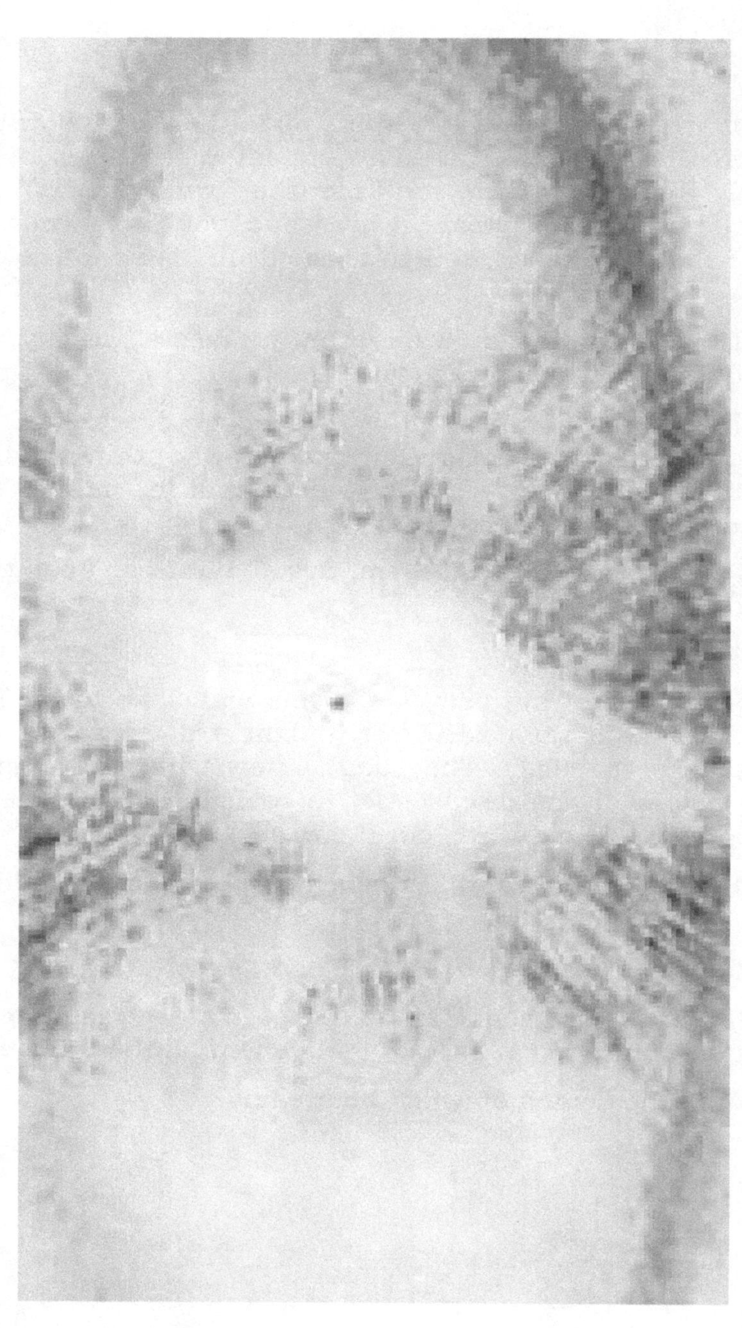

3.

affordability (absent)

there are things
you can't afford

drinking
for instance

I never drink

some do
but not me

my head
is always
clear

friendship
falls into the same
boat

dependencies
are a problem

I thought about a dog
at one time
but no
it wouldn't work

there are so many things
in the world
that seem almost
designed
to weaken a man

that can't be allowed
to happen

The game is on, never off. Always listening, always learning, always knowing how the world turns. Take no chances, bear no witness.

To be invisible is what it takes. A slip, any loose moment, either awake or asleep, in bed or in play, in thought or in deed – can't happen. Won't happen. The job is all there is now, and this game is nothing short of life and death.

My life, her life. All others are bound for death. If she wills it.

Her will, my word to follow her way.

There are rules, too, and I know them well.

Who showed her how to hunt, how to find prey, how to show the error of their ways? If I was the teacher, and she was the student, when did she become the Master and place me as her Apprentice?

After the first time, that's when.

The broken little bird I found, the one I took back to my lair in the hidden places, she grew. Not in body, but in spirit.

The stories I read to her while she healed, the stories of life and lust and justice, she took them on like a badge, like the wings of her magnificent steed. My Herja became the deepest meaning of her soul.

Justice. Vengeance. She takes back the life of those who take lives. There is no leeway when it comes to the rules.

Obey, be the purpose of her judgement, and be the one, the only. There can be no others before her, higher or lower. None can walk by my side.

I am the follower, the shadow of her weights and measures, the loom for her weft and weave that decides the fate of those who knot the thread.

One purpose exists, one only. My heart is full.

rapture

I use a rod

some micro-fabric
on a jag
and solvents

a special
brush

the full kit
when I'm at home

on the road
I make do

toothbrush
and some soft cloths

most hardware stores
will have enough
of what I need
to attend my cleaning

I can spend
a whole evening
every day
when I have the time

pulling apart

rubbing down

brushing
and polishing

putting back together

cleaning a weapon
can be like
a meditation
for me

a higher place
where I can visualise
uses

actions
and effects

visualizing the thing
is like being the thing

I'm not religious
no
not at all

but
the business of existing
in a higher state
is a real thing
for me

a kind of
rapture

Music haunts the movements of my actions. The tools are ready, always ready, for her word to come. Clean. A good tool is always on the bench, clean and assembled.

What music do I hear? Is it the dense orchestral sounds of the ride? Something newer, more cutting? Each must fit the purpose. Not of the name, but of the tool. Each tool has a soul, a memory of what it can do, what it has done.

I am one with the tools.

Each implement is one of two. It is a matter of professionalism. Always be ready. Always have the best instrument for the job.

One can be on the bench, one must be ready to go. Nothing left out, nothing to be seen, not here.

Only the beating of my heart, the pulse pounding, the body as much a weapon, sharper.

For each weapon, each tool, is a process. Touch this, smooth that, sharpen edges, toughen burls or remove a notch – or two.

What do I hear as the stone caresses the blade? Is it the sound of her hair bunched into a plait? Or the whisper and scowl of leather as the jacket slides over her shoulders?

Reminds me to oil up the sheaths, prepare the dusting powder for the hidden pouches, the secret fanny packs for the specialist equipment.

Each piece has its place. Each box or drawer or receptacle contains the right tool for one job, at least one job.

Each tool must be maintained at the peak of preparedness for its designed purpose.

And I am one tool in the swag.

up and down

it's like
hot
and cold

on
and off

if you're going
to survive
and thrive
you have to be able
to make the shift
in your own mental state

when you're
stood down
it has to be
as if stood down
is what
you've always been

when you're up
though

that's all
there is

Sometimes, there's a catch in my chest, a pain. Where it comes from ... I can't say.

Is it excitement? Fear? More? Less?

What do I know?

The tool is no more than the will of the bearer.

Let's not think about it, I say to the little lump in there. Do, or be done. The rules are simple. Do the job, do it right, leave nothing behind.

The deepest meaning – bring nothing of the soul to the job. Leave that behind, but maybe carry the torment, the pain of body and mind, brought to bear by those who wouldn't wish it on themselves.

I am that reflection, I am the self they fear.

Doesn't matter where I come from, where they come from, only the tracks left, or the light that shines without hindrance.

Or the shadow that stretches beyond the grip of those who try to escape.

I am the mirror.

Do I see myself in there somewhere?

It makes no difference. Do, and be done with it. I am her dotted 'i' and crossed 't', no more than that.

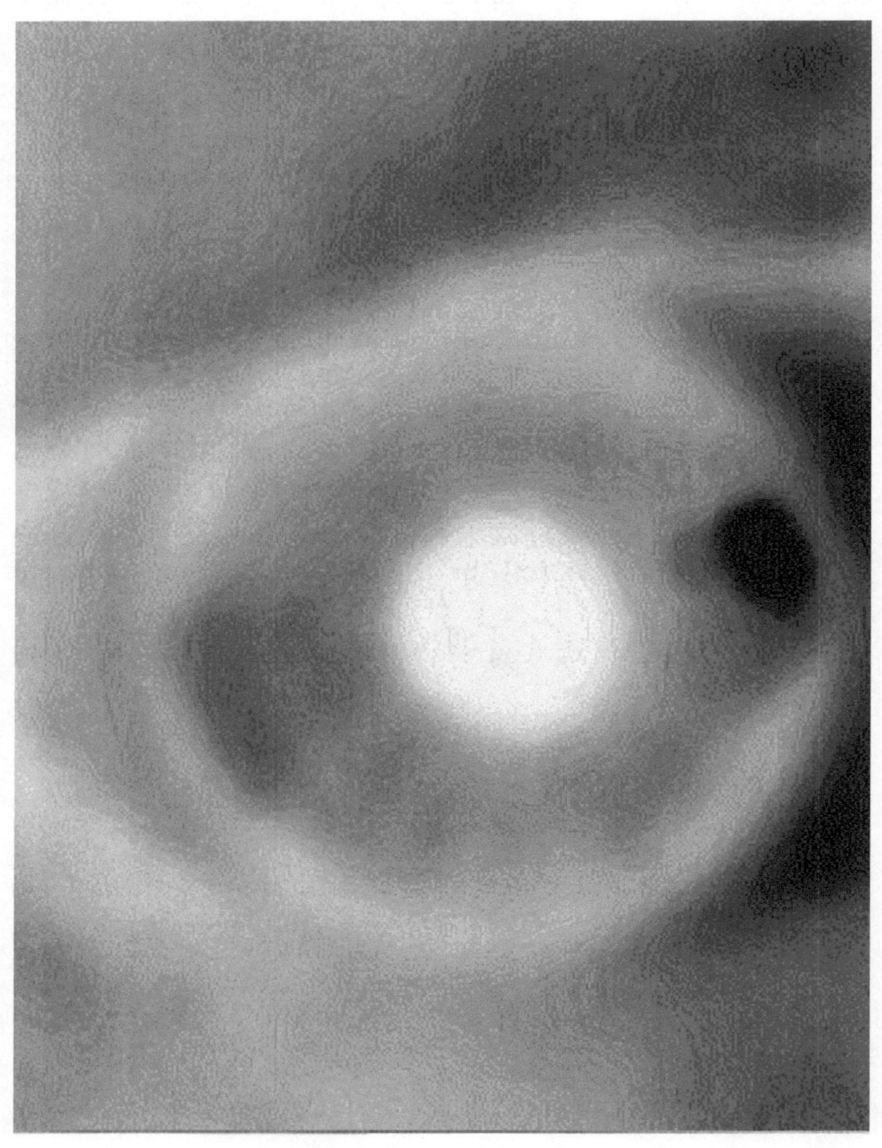

4.

unavailable (by phone)

I travel a lot

when I'm working

when I'm not
working

I get restless
when I've got
nothing much
to do

so
I travel

look around

you have to have
a phone these days
you know

a device
they call them

but
here's the thing
in my work
I can't have a phone

the government
traces
phones

it's not just
my paranoia
no
they really do it
the government

they listen
and they track

and they follow

so
I have a device
a chinese or indian thing
but
it's no phone

I use it
to take pictures
that's all

when I need
to touch base
about once
every week or so

I go to a shop
log in
anonymous

punch in a url
that I know
in my head

and after
I kill the memory

walk away

the government
has got its work cut out
tracking me

What is it called? That word where what is seen isn't what's there? Yeah, that one. It's the best tool in my kit. Wanna know it?

Obfuscate.

People think that what they see is real, that the things they see are only what they appear to be. There is more. And less.

I carry the phone, but it's not a phone. I use it as if it worked. It doesn't. The camera clicks, the sounds happen, but there's no sim, so there's no tracer in there.

I remain as unseen as a man can be.

In each group of people I'm with, I bring out one of my others, and he plays with them, talks with them, speaks their lingo.

I can parrot any lingo, any idiom.

If what you expected from what I do is that it only comes from below, that the streets spawn what I am – dead wrong.

tainted air

no
I don't do what you might call
personal
work

just business

I mean
you can't just go around
doing
what I do
to settle a grudge
or to score
some sort of point

it's easier
smarter
to keep your head
down
and your nose clean

that's my motto

it's funny
though

over the journey
I've found less
trouble
coming my way
at a personal level

it's like
the air around me
has changed
over the years

people seem to feel
me
in their space
like a sniff
of danger
and they give me
extra room
without them even knowing
why

I think it must be
a taint
in the atmosphere
that travels around
with me

the taint of what I do

There's music, you know, that comes at the right time. It pounds into the blood like a tonic or a boon, and then it dances the body, or it tempts the brain to think or sing or dance.

My music is different.

It has blades, sharp blades for the quick dispatchment, dull blades for the ones who need to suffer longer, jagged blades to mess 'em up.

Long and short and thin and thick and wide and narrow. Blades have music, when they swing through the air or saw through the solidity of life.

The guns have more than sound and touch. They have a smell in their music. Not just one aroma, but many.

The enveloping perfumes in the shed, doing maintenance, the smell in the field when I unwrap them from their hides, the smell of their power when used for purpose.

The hammer, the tongs, the pincers – they have more of a sound than a smell, but that sound is energising with the other side of the game. They smell of fear, but sound like plain vanilla. Sliced vanilla, of course!

What? Not funny? It is, you know.

How would you rather go? Fast or slow, sharp or blunt, close or distant?

It won't matter of course, but if you smell me coming, you better move.

And you will smell it, you will hear it, the music will come for you when your name is on my job list.

No music will save you then, no sky-riders will come for you.

How do I know?

You have to earn the right, you have to do the job without question, you have to bear the stink of it.

Then she'll come for you, to drag you from the field of gore.

Whether you go to the big table, to battle for justice ever-after – or whether you go to the fields of peace ... not up to you, is it? Never has been, never will be.

It is what it is, and only Herja knows the beat of your song.

any colour darkness

well black
of course

it makes sense
don't you think

shirt
jacket
pants
shoes

it just makes sense

this business of mine
isn't flower arranging

or bright colours

you think about it
you'll find yourself
drifting
straightaway
toward the night
and shadows

and darkness

Silly little buggers. Black? The man in black, you say?

It's how I see you when you play at being me, at being the scary shadow.

But black isn't black, is it?

Look at the night-sky sometime, but be outta town when you do, and see what there is to see. Not black, of that you can be sure. Not black.

What you see is – now, you gotta be lucky sometimes – the shimmer of an aurora, the blues and greens and reds and silvers of each star, each creature of the night sky. And the moon! Boy, is that a dead giveaway that there's no true black.

Wanna know why you don't see me coming? I can tell you now, it ain't because I'm black or wearing black or painted black – it's because I fit in.

Camo – that's what it is. The difference between the pretender and the man is the difference between the shadow and the shade.

Some might not see it, but I do, because I am your shadow, and even if you think you hide in the shade, there's a deeper shadow – and it's right on your heels.

Silly buggers play the game of black.

And I ain't silly.

5.

I, camera

it's like
being the camera

the lens sees
what the picture
becomes

it makes the scene
that it sees

but
you look at the picture
and
you never actually see
the camera

I'm the camera

I
make the scene
that becomes
the picture

The face is blurred on the screen when they try to run, moving too fast for the camera to focus well. But I see, I move with them, I unblur the movement. I am the camera, it is my eye that centres the picture, that frames the moment. I'm here, now, and the final frame is set.

Often, it's not my camera that sends the confirmation. Why make myself visible? I use the device they carry, and send the pic to the cloud.

Cloud? What a word to use for someone's – I'll never say the who or what; I know who's watching and listening – memory storage farm.

My cloud? The one I use isn't mine. It's a public space, and the only trace to the pic I load, the one that pops up for the requisite three seconds as confirmation or warning, is the device I use. Not mine.

And if they see it, if they come, if they see the message in that space, they know it's a job.

It's a case of professional ethics that leads me to shape and stage the setting, to make sure that any who choose to follow in the steps, who ignore the warning given, will know what end comes.

Will they know why?

They should, if they know him – oh, I apologise, if they knew him – if they were party to what he did to catch her attention.

Pay heed, people. If you think the enemy who watches is the one who cannot act, see this – and think again, or wait your turn. It only takes her word.

hammer (the same)

well
you know
when they say

if a man's tool
is a hammer
every problem
looks like
a nail

that's me

I'm the guy
with a hammer

all my problems
get treated
the same

A blunt instrument is a blunt instrument.

A hammer is a hammer.

A tool is a tool.

But a tool is only as good as the maintenance it receives.

All my tools, every hammer and clamp and bench, every wrench and grip and saw, every tool is in its place, is treated to care and attention. Twenty minutes on each tool, each week, otherwise, the hammer slips or the saw catches or the clamp threads.

I am the tool, and she is my maintenance. I am given the task. She keeps my motivation strong, my skills sharp, my mind alert and aware.

I am a hammer, but not any hammer. The hammer in the hand of the sister to the Valkyrie, the hammer of Herja, Devastation.

I am hers, body and soul and craft.

to pray (or not)

first impressions
are important

I always judge

you'd think
it might be
a difficult
thing

so many different
people

personalities

backgrounds

motivations

but no
that's not the way of it
for me

when I look
at a person
I just ask
myself

victim?
not victim?

like a tiger
or some other big cat
deciding

prey?
or not prey?

that's all

'The clothes make the man,' they say. The way he walks, too. The things he does, the things he collects, the way he uses words. The places he likes to be, the people he surrounds himself with.

All these things make the man – or woman. They shape themselves into packages to meet some unknown inner need.

I don't see that, but I use it to my advantage.

Every hunter must know the ways of his prey.

Patience is what it takes. A true predator requires patience, time to watch and wait and measure the tread.

Survival, mine, not theirs, is what it's about. Prey animals may be wary, but there are times the guard is down.

It is wordless, a picture they scratch out into their world, their shape, their patterns. Patterns attract my eye, my nose, my training.

Is it a skill, I wonder, or a calling? Would I have found this purpose if not for the horror of her downfall?

Did a higher power call upon me that day, did it ask me to become capable again in the service of his judge, and I as the executioner of that arm?

Hunter, is what I am, execute orders, is what I do. I seek them out, in their dens, in their travels, in their holes, and I sniff at their desperation, the desire to live one more day, to complete tasks or say farewells or ... some want only to do it one more time.

However, it is not my call to make. I serve. I am her compliant servant, and I act for a higher will, a stronger resolve – or is what I feel pleasure when I complete a task that brings a smile to her face, as I imagine it sometimes, at the conclusion of a job done well?

6.

the way of it

sometimes
it's months

one time
a year
and a half

just lately
there's been something
to do
almost every week

that's the way
it moves

Love is something that grows.

It takes time and patience. I have those things in abundance. I have shapelessness and flexibility and intent.

Love is what keeps me here, even knowing there will be an end.

There are rules, you know. Rules. I know the rules.

Okay, one rule.

I know that rule.

Have I kept to the rule, and not just the letter of the law of it?

We shall see, we shall indeed see.

I wait.

Like every other job that comes in, I wait.

never a chance

it's a life
of lies

that
is what it comes down to

the thing with
love

see
there's an issue there
straight away

the *problem*
with love
is that it seems to require
honesty

some honesty
and a lot
of sharing

can you imagine

what did you do
at work today
dear ...

no
I don't even try
to do that
anymore

it's like I told you
I'm good
I'm really good
alone

Pain is all that remains. It's in my memories. The before.

It's not before now. Now is not emptiness, as it was before. Now is more than any one person can imagine big enough. Now is the real me.

I sense the emptiness, though, the one to come.

What if it went away? That's the one that brings on the feelings, the aloneness that goes beyond the void. What if she didn't need me anymore? What if I failed to meet the expectations?

Worse, what if I bungled a job?

Would I know about it?

Would there be a stab in the back?

I left a message once, when one of the empty days came.

'I am the last contract,' I wrote, and I know she'll understand.

What life would I have if not this? It would be cold and beyond lonely, lost to the way of before if not for the man I am now, the one who changed from lost and useless to the one who understands desire and pleasure. Her pleasure is my exaltation.

If that were lost ...

light up

want a smoke

it's ok
I know
you're a smoker

I don't mind

and
it's not as though
it'll damage your health

not
this one

go ahead

light up

There are smokers and there are chokers.

I like the smokers. Sometimes, if they share one with me, I might let them have the last gasp.

What harm, I ask you? What harm now?

And when he takes the last gasp, or gurgle, or huff, I make sure I take his puff.

Nothing like a beer and a smoke when a man gets home from a big job.

Of course, I don't drink and I don't smoke. Both those things make a man stink, make him visible when he needs to be invisible, but after the job's done ... what harm?

Eh?

Wanna puff? A last puff, of course ...

7.

do

I don't know
how it turned out
that I could do
this job

I heard someone say
one time
that maybe you can only do some work
if you have
a calling

without the calling
you just couldn't
do it

wouldn't
consider it

I don't know

it's not like
I had
a childhood apprenticeship
with animals

or set fire
to anything

I just could

I just did

I just
do

It's a question someone always asks.

They talk about it sometimes, wonder if they could. I know most couldn't, even in the worst circumstance. Some could, but they'd be the thugs, the heavies – often these are my targets, so it goes to show, right?

Some think a trained soldier could do it, but they have morals, it's why they're soldiers, and not mercenaries.

I'm not a merc. I'm not a thug or a heavy or a lout.

You know why I can do it?

Not because I have no heart, but the opposite. Because I helped someone who needed it. And then I helped her become what she needed to be.

In turn, she helped me become the best me, to use the skills of the street, the stresses of the life before, and use them to exact not just justice and measure, but to see my true inner self.

Not a black heart, nor even grey. My heart is red, fire like a volcano, banked, the releases are timed, given as retribution.

The ones I end know why I'm there. They know this is the price of their actions.

They did, I do.

I do it for the bound woman, the woman beaten almost to death, who came back with fire in her soul and justice in her offer.

I can do it because she asks it of me, and that's the only reason.

not all that funny

me?

no
I don't tell
jokes

oh
I know some

I know
plenty

some good ones
too

but
no

I can be funny
all right
but when it's me
the kind of funny
that it is . . .

is like
a heart attack

I'm not really
a laughing matter

Bugger the funny. It's no joke to me. Not in words, nor any other way it could be perceived. Not funny at all.

I could give reasons, I could blame.

It's what they do. They try to justify.

Why do they need to tell me, to beg forgiveness?

Not mine to give, I say, nor to ask. Too late, I say, all I do is take, that's all.

To look too hard, to ask the wrong way, to let others too deep inside, that's irony.

They look at last, and realise, and some laugh.

Not me.

The contract, the value given to the payment I take on for them.

It's no joke.

what part

you know
I wonder
from time to time
about the
why
of it

what happened

how did it come
to this

who got so mad
that they asked for
me
.
.
.

.
but
it's not my job
to know

not my job
to care
either

I'm just the end
of a long arm
reaching out to finish
a certain piece
of business

the part that sorts
what needs
to be sorted

Down the drub the other day, and listen to blokes being blokes.

They don't see the real me, of course. I'm the bushie poet who comes in to beg for a feed, a down-trodden old fart with a long bushie beard and a stink of six feet under – or worse.

I'm not setting up, not while I'm here, not in these moments. But I wonder, I do often wonder, why it came to me this way.

I only did one good thing in my life, and that one moment led me into this life. To be the hand of justice means not asking questions, not digging beyond the need to fulfil the contract, to give the 'paid in full' message at the end of each job.

What if life had been what my father wanted?

The life of easy, he called it. Well-educated men go on to become this or that, they have plenty and do more and …

Not for me, it seems. It broke me.

Nah, I wasn't the only one. There are plenty of us on the hidden laneways, the dirty streets, behind or inside blinds, sneaking down streets before the garbo comes through.

When I was still one of them, I'd find the ones who did the recitations, and we'd sit there the night through, speak the words, imagine another life.

But I was the one who took the chance when it came.

It's all I am now, all I can be.

8.

I don't fly

nope
never

did it
once or twice
and couldn't let go
of the armrests

teeth clenched
and eyes closed
the whole way

a guy
like me
can't go around
with his eyes
closed

and I hated it

take off

and
especially
the landing

I see enough
of mortality
without having to
imagine
it

The rules for me are different to hers. I have some, not many, but one in particular.

I don't go up there. I make my own way, travel wherever in the country she wants me to go. No offshore, no boats, no skipping across the ditch.

No high-rise buildings, at least, nothing higher than seven floors – a man could survive a fall from seven floors! Maybe it wouldn't be a good survival, but at least I could say goodbye, somehow, get a message to the right site.

No trains, either. How can a man locked in a moving tin-can use his mind? It's not possible. Not possible at all. I can't do it. No trains, no trams, no taxi-cabs or those other things.

Take out all the things that change the level of control a man with a job needs, and these become what damages and risks the outcome.

I don't fly. I don't swim, I got no wings, nor do I get stuck in small spaces.

It makes me shudder.

The people I see, they see, they socialise, they smile. They can do these things, smile like idiots while they're confined in small spaces. Not me. Never me.

When I go to the drub, I make sure they stay as far away as possible. I make sure the door is real close and people are real far.

I sing and dance and speak from next to the door, ready to run.

Not for the reasons they think, not for the reasons any normal person would think.

I just don't like being hemmed in, confined, unable to control the environment.

A hunter doesn't get inside the trap. Not unless he's old or got a death wish.

fullstop

well
you know
sometimes
it has to be done
with heft

never mind
what you feel
more comfortable with

certain situations . . .
certain times . . .

a blunt instrument
swung hard
is a full stop

and the sentence
is finished

just like . . .

that

There's a certain magic to the way words make sense.

Each sentence has a structure – a subject, a verb, and an object.

The subject of my sentence is the name on the list.

He or she or it will be fed a verb.

What will the verb be?

The tool she sets out is the verb. Act with this, in this way, is what it says without the need for more than the verb itself.

And the object, in this case, the blunt object, means … here's the fullstop, bud.

A dead-stop, period, fullstop.

none

it's funny
when I think
about it

I'm a man
who knows
no one

wherever I go
I meet people

I meet
a lot
of people

we spend
a little time
you know

but
when I leave

there's no one

I make sure
that there is
no one

It used to be called something different.

Alone, or left alone, or being alone. Choice or circumstance. Fear or failure or licking the wounds.

Alone.

I get real close to some of the names.

I do. I can get real chatty.

Know why?

When I let him know why he's my friend of the moment, and where I'll be tomorrow, he – or she or it – forgets the mask.

It's a wonderful thing to see, I tell you. A real person lies under all the glib stuff, and that may be the only time the person sees himself as he really is.

I smile then, 'cos I know the real me. I've seen that darkness, and I returned.

Yeah, okay, I didn't do it on my own. I had her, but these guys had their options, too, and they chose different.

Now their choices are slim, none, gone.

'Bye,' I says, at the end.

9.

chances are

the way I see it
there's always
a chance

you know

maybe
you'd say
no
to that
but
you're wrong

I always figure
I could miss

it's happened before

once

so
yeah

there's always
a chance

It was only the once, mind you, that the job didn't finish as
it should.

Once is all it takes.

That's why there are always two bullets with the rifle, a
full clip, or two blades. A garrote is backup to the blade or
the hammer.

Mistakes happen.

Once.

angel

I don't like
names

usually
I only want to know
one name

more than that
confuses my emotions

why would I
want to know
the wife
or the husband

or the kids names

it just makes them
into people

you know

I don't want
people
in my head

me?

you can call me
anything you like

call me
angel
if you want

you?

I'm going to call you
target

that's all the names
someone like me
needs
to know

The naming of a thing makes it real.

A bird isn't a bird 'cos it's got wings. A dog isn't a dog 'cos it can bark.

A man like me isn't a monster 'cos of what he does.

A turn of phrase can burn or brand, a connotation can blame and shame, but look in that mirror, you see you and I see me, am I a man because I think I am?

My angel comes for me.

Why is she an angel? Why does that name apply to my Herja?

Have you seen her fly down on her wild steed, have you seen how she reaches down and inflicts death on the enemy, and benediction on the favoured?

No?

I have. I was the hand of benediction.

Was.

Funny word.

It has named me.

It was in the message.

Was.

I have to find a way to enact that word, to make a transitive verb of it.

It has to become me.

The naming of a thing makes it real, you know.

The rule. I know the rule.

Knew the rule.

Missed the mark.

Saw it clear.

It's coming, the thought said.

The word that came to me, the verb of my end, the message on wings – end.

This will be my end.

The word said it to my reflection, my real self.

the power (of thought)

I try
not to think
too much

someone
like me
has powerful thoughts

you know
you do what I do
and even your thoughts
get charged

super charged

I've heard
the expression

kill a man
with a look

but
I'm old fashioned

I like to give my hands
something to do

and I try
not to think
too hard

The sounds in the street, in the air. Birds and trees and wind and movement.

They're not for me, not now.

I use words to make my way. Words to sway people, to mask the man beneath. Not now.

The slip came, it was always coming. It came.

The end is nigh, so it says. Not the end, though, just mine.

And there's a choice in there.

It's the chance to take a shot at integrity, at honour, at offering my resignation.

Can I say what I feel? Don't you know?

Doesn't the wind through her hair say it to her every day?

The mirror I have is not me, it is not the man I am.

In that mirror, in the soul that underlies mine, is her face, battered and bruised, bleeding and broken.

That is the face I see in the mirror.

Her face.

I need words to get me past that.

But now my word has ended, and into the night I go.

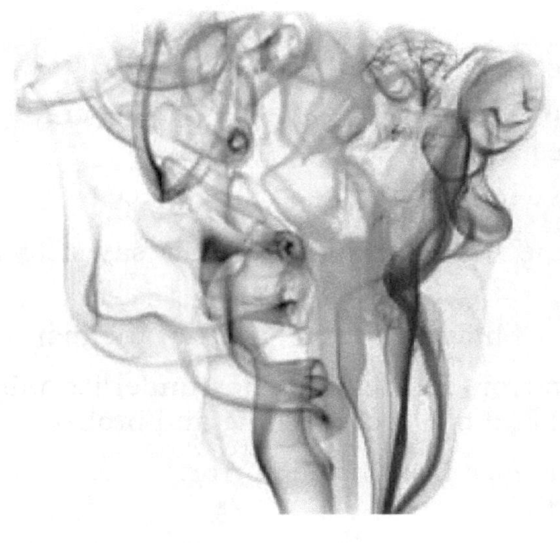

10.

silence

and here
the field is white
like snow

the colour of my hand
my face
pale now
and clean

as though purified

me
waiting
in silence

the end . . .

she comes

When I give my word, it's the word I speak that's true and strong, not a word given and forgotten. It's my promise.

To earn trust, even in the putrid spaces of dank dreams, the places we both came from, is the bond we share. Stronger than faith, than blood, or words on paper bonds.

The word is given, and once given, silence and the nod is all that's required. Anything more distorts the view, the underlying contract. She, my Herja, gives me the name and the tool, and I know, I understand. No more words are required.

Devastation comes, and she shows you her weapon. I am that.

Silence.

Be silent at the end. Show acceptance.

Who doesn't know what is coming when the warning is given?

They all know. I don't tell them, I don't ask. I never ask why. Nor how. The tools show how she wants to see it done.

I do.

All I ask is silence, no screaming like a little kid in tantrum mode. It's too late now. Take the message, take it with you.

so

so

anyway

it's time

The last job. It came today. Expected it.

The white background, black text. Finale, it said without using the word. The word I saw – 'was' alongside the name I used to wear. The man with the childhood. The man who wasn't me, hadn't been me for so long because he wasn't a real person, just a hope for someone else.

Now ... now ... I must choose a tool. She didn't leave one.

That's a message, too. My choice. Clean and neat, or nasty and messy.

But I'm professional. I'll take the best tool, the one that won't lead anywhere, and I'll take this body and I'll go elsewhere ...

But my mind will never clear. I will never forget, even beyond this world, I will swear myself to her service.

That day, that afternoon so long ago – or so it seems, now – when I dragged her out of the gutter they threw her in, that's the day my life began.

I took her to my safe place, the old shed.

I picked her up, patched her up, fed her up – how could I help what it made between us?

Still, I owe a life to the one who takes it all at the end, and I won't let her down, I won't beg, I won't offer to start again.

I'll smile, I'll doff that hat I never wear except on a job, and I'll take the next step alone.

'See ya, then,' I'll say. 'But not too soon.'

Live long, is what I send to the message board. Live long, feel real is what I send with my heart.

I bow and exit, stage left, curtains come down.

fade

someone comes

someone so black
that I am . . .
not anything

not anywhere

I am

not

We all die. It's a given. Sooner or later, we die. When death comes for you, how will you greet him?

I greet him as a friend, with open arms, and open eyes, for I have seen true justice. I have borne the sword for the one who holds my life and my light, and I do for her whatever she asks.

True justice, you see, has value more than life. And unlike death, justice does not come to all, and many escape the slippery lines justice tries to hook into the conscience of those who stray from the line.

Not I. I remember it all. We're all going to die, is what I've said to many, and now to myself.

I die willingly, with joy, for I have been the hand of justice, the scales, the weight.

We all die. We die, and now I die well, and hope she finds the words I scribbled in her honour, in her name. Not her human name, the name of her justice, the name Herja, Devastation.

I die with joy in my soul, with love in my heart.

About the Authors

Frank Prem has been a storytelling poet for forty years. When not writing or reading his poetry to an audience, he fills his time by working as a psychiatric nurse.

He has been published in magazines, zines and anthologies, in Australia and in a number of other countries, and has both performed and recorded his work as 'spoken word'.

Frank has released two collections of free verse poetry:
Small Town Kid (Dec 2018)and
Devil In The Wind (May 2019)

He and his wife live in the beautiful township of Beechworth in northeast Victoria (Australia).

Frank Prem Contacts and Social Media

Author Page (Newsletter sign up): https://FrankPrem.com

Facebook page: https://www.facebook.com/frankprem2

YouTube: https://
www.youtube.com/channel/UCvfW2WowqY1euO-Cj76LDKg

Twitter: https://twitter.com/frank_prem

Amazon: https://www.amazon.com/-/e/B07L61HNZ4

Goodreads: https://
www.goodreads.com/author/show/18679262.Frank_Prem

* * *

Cage Dunn is honest about being a fibber, fabricator and teller of tall tales. Oh, and a storyteller.
Cage lives with a dog, a garden, and a mind that's never at home. Find the blog (and books) at:

www.cagedunn.wordpress.com
https://www.bookbub.com/authors/cage-dunn
https://www.amazon.com/Cage-Dunn/e/B01DBJFSQC

Other works:

Diaballein, horror
The Old Woman & the Mad Horse, thriller/suspense
Who Will Rule Magic? Kraken, Dragon, Cat vs. Kangaroo, Cockatoo, Crocodile, fantasy allegory
Not on the Cards, Urban Fantasy, Arcane
Seeking, anthology

www.ingramcontent.com/pod-product-compliance
Lightning Source LLC
Chambersburg PA
CBHW030647190726
48286CB00008B/2691